For my dear Mother Dear

Balzer + Bray is an imprint of HarperCollins Publishers.

Samson: The Piranha Who Went to Dinner
Copyright © 2017 by Tadgh Bentley
All rights reserved. Printed in China.

ISBN 978-0-06-233537-1

All illustrations for this book were drawn using pen and ink and colored digitally

Typography by Ellice M. Lee
16 17 18 19 20 SCP 10 9 8 7 6 5 4 3 2 1
❖
First Edition

SAMSON
The Piranha Who Went to Dinner

Tadgh Bentley

BALZER + BRAY
An Imprint of HarperCollins Publishers

Samson was a rather adventurous fellow.

While other piranhas stayed close to home, he wanted to explore far and wide. And while they stuck to the same old routine,

Samson liked to get out and try new things.

Excuse me, would you like to play a game of tennis?
No!

How about a trip upstream?
NO!

Most of all, Samson dreamed
of eating fine food at the
fanciest restaurants.

But while he drooled
at the thought of
luscious lily linguine
and crispy kelp cakes,

the other piranhas ate the
same boring food
day
after
day.

So every day Samson ate alone. Until one morning he saw something he thought might change their minds. . . .

FISHY TIMES
FANCY
RESTAURANTS
OPEN TODAY

Fancy restaurants! Opening today! Perhaps you gents might care to join me for a—
No way!
Not for me!
Silly Samson—a restaurant is no place for a piranha!
FISH TIMES
FANCY RESTAURANTS
OPEN TODAY

Perhaps they were right.
With their fearsome features and terrible
teeth, piranhas weren't really welcome
anywhere, let alone in fancy restaurants.

But he had to try.
So Samson set off alone . . .
and soon arrived at the
first restaurant.

He smiled his friendliest smile and approached the waiter.

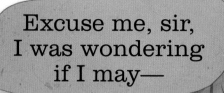

His friends were right. He couldn't get into a restaurant looking like a piranha.

But maybe he COULD get in looking like something else. He would need a disguise!

Samson checked his moustache and fluffed his eyebrows. He could almost taste the luscious lily linguine and the sizzling seaweed sausages!

Pardon me, but I believe you have a reservation for Samson P. Rana?
LINGUINE'S

Let me see. . . . Of course, Mr. Rana. Right this way, please. . . .

Samson peered eagerly into the
restaurant. And when he saw the plates
piled high with crispy kelp cakes and
duckweed sauce, he couldn't help but
smile a large, very piranha-like smile.

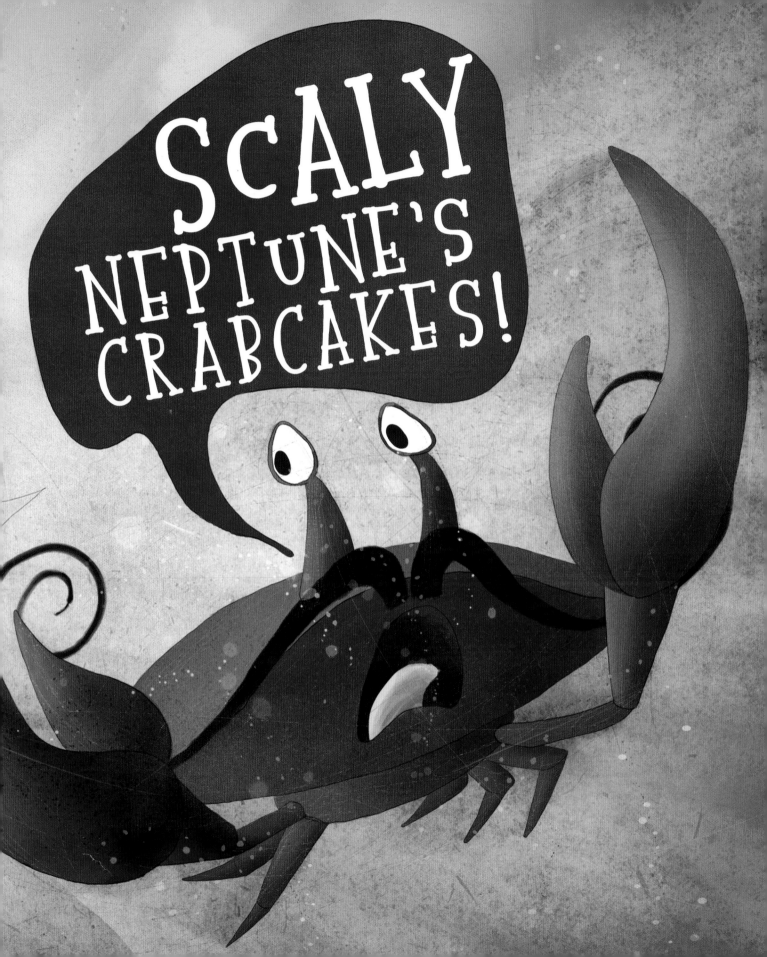

Samson's smile
disappeared
as fast as the fish
in the restaurant.

He couldn't get into a restaurant,
and he didn't fit in at home.

Samson felt more alone than ever.

There was only one more restaurant,
one more chance for a fancy meal.
This time he would make sure his
costume was perfect.

"This is it," thought Samson.

He nervously swam up to the final restaurant.

Excuse me, my name is Mr. Rana, and I have a reservation for this evening.

Ah, Monsieur Rana, of course. Right this way, please. . . .

Would you like to sample some creamy crab soufflé? Or perhaps some crispy kelp cakes?

Samson's mouth watered.
Had he finally made it?

Please, sir, allow me to take your hat.

Samson couldn't believe it. His dream was about to come true! But just then . . .

FOR THE LOVE OF SMOKY SEA BASS!

But this time, as fish scattered this way and that, taking their delicious kelp cakes and soufflés with them, Samson realized . . .

he wasn't the only fearsome fish who wanted to dine out on fancy food.

And, with his new friends, came a new idea.
They would open their own fancy restaurant—
one where the food was so good that this time,

it wasn't Samson
wearing a disguise.